ʃƐX EXPLAINED

SƐXEXPLAINED

honest answers to your questions about guys & girls,
your changing body, and what really happens during sex

Magali Clausener-Petit with Melissa Daly
illustrated by Soledad

sunscreen

Book series designed by Higashi Glaser Design

Library of Congress Cataloging-in-Publication data has been applied for.

ISBN: 0-8109-9162-4

Text copyright © 2004 Magali Clausener-Petit with Melissa Daly
Illustrations copyright © 2003 Soledad

Translated by Paul Hurwit

AMULET

Published in 2004 by Amulet Books
an imprint of Harry N. Abrams, Incorporated
100 Fifth Avenue
New York, NY 10011
www.abramsbooks.com

Printed and bound in China
10 9 8 7 6 5 4 3 2 1

Abrams is a subsidiary of
LA MARTINIÈRE

To my parents, who always answered
my questions about sexuality.

— M.C.P.

To Pascal for his loving support.

— S

contents

phase 3:

phase 4:

WHAT EXACTLY IS GOING ON INSIDE MY BODY? WHAT'S AN ERECTION? WHERE DOES MENSTRUAL BLOOD COME FROM? HOW DO YOU HAVE SEX? HOW OLD DO I HAVE TO BE TO KNOW I'M IN LOVE?

Questions like these have probably been nagging at you for a while now. Those videos they show in health class just never seem to explain all the different things you're wondering about—and there's no way you're going to raise your hand and ask in front of everyone!

In addition to living in a body that seems to change more every day, you're also probably experiencing new sensations and new desires—in other words, you're discovering sexuality. And you're getting more and more curious about some of the words you've been hearing: ejaculation, masturbation, orgasm...the list goes on. You wish someone would just explain straight out what really happens between two people when they have sex.

It's hard to talk about this subject with any adult, let alone your parents. As for your friends, they don't have the answers to everything (well, not the right ones anyway). That's precisely why we wrote this book—to answer your questions about sex and your body, no matter how embarrassing they may seem to you.

SEXUALITY

a voyage deep inside the body

sex = life

THE SPERM'S WILD RIDE

a baby is born

THE METAMORPHOSIS

AND LIFE

sex=life

most of you already have a good idea of where babies come from. They don't just miraculously appear inside their mothers' bellies. You know that the sex organs, sexual intercourse, and, in short, everything covered by the word "sexuality" somehow explain how babies are born. And yet you may find it hard to actually picture what happens when a man has sex with a woman. Physically, though, it's fairly straightforward: the man inserts his sexual organ, the penis, into the woman's sexual organ, the vagina. This is called "penetration." But when people say the word "sex," they usually mean much more than just penetration. Sex is also about the kissing, touching, and caressing that two people do before, during, and after penetration.

Sex is a natural part of life. And since it is such a natural thing, it's not surprising that you hear a lot of talk about sex and sexuality. After all, it's pretty important for a lot of reasons. For one thing, it gives pleasure. For another, it allows two people to show that they love each other with their actions, not just with words. And sex is essential because it enables human beings to reproduce by having children. In other words, without sex, there'd be no reproduction, no birth, no children, and, ultimately, no life.

This baby-making stuff is no sweat!

a tale of

When a man **and a woman** make a baby, it's often a conscious choice. They want a child because they love each other, and what's more, they want their love story to extend beyond their own lives. They want to give life in the same way that they received it. They've made this decision because they feel the desire to "reproduce," or, in other words, to make another human being. They may also want a child for reasons they sometimes don't even suspect: to be able to stand up as parents themselves alongside their own mother and father, to experience the incredible love a parent has for a child and a child has for his or her parents—in other words, to create a family.

For all of these reasons, both conscious and unconscious, conceiving a child is a true adventure for a man and a woman. And it all starts inside their own bodies.

You'll see very quickly how important the simple act of *meeting* is in creating new life. You yourself were born because of a special meeting: when your mother met your father. And you were conceived thanks to another special meeting: when an ovum met a sperm.

But these two microscopic cells—the ovum and the sperm—go through a lot before their meeting can ever happen. To find out their stories, we have to look deep inside the human body.

two people

Look, I'd like us to get married, to have a lot of kids, a big house, two, maybe three dogs . . .

I'd just like a coffee.

The Female Sex Organs

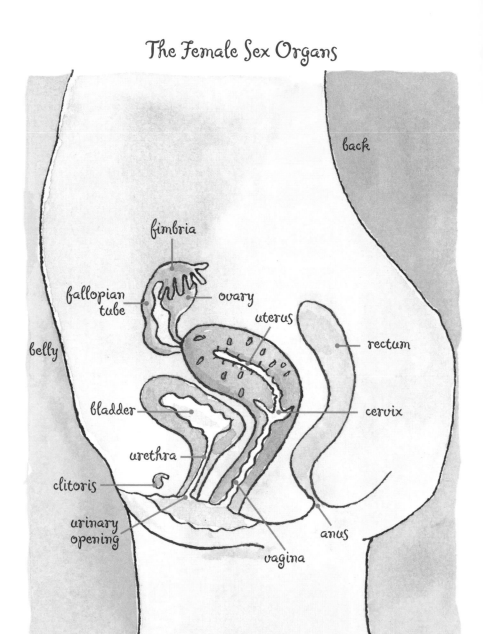

cross section

the female star

In this tale, the female star is the ovum. The ovum is the woman's sex cell. Every girl reaches puberty with about 300,000 to 400,000 ova (that's just the word for more than one ovum) stored in her two ovaries.✣ Until puberty arrives, the ova lie quietly inside the ovaries doing pretty much nothing.

But then puberty delivers a sort of wake-up call to the ova. When a girl reaches a certain age, hormones✳ inside her body trigger a process called the menstrual cycle, in which the ova play a starring role. This cycle of events normally lasts for twenty-eight days and then repeats itself. Over the course of the month, one ovum matures, or grows, inside one of the two ovaries. When it reaches maturity, the ovum emerges and floats away from the ovary. This process is called ovulation. After the ovum leaves the ovary, it is swept up inside one of the fallopian tubes, the two small ducts that connect the ovaries to the uterus, or womb. The ovum's big scene now begins, for it's here, in this long, narrow canal leading to the uterus, that the ovum may meet up with the sperm of its dreams.

✣ OVARIES·
The ova, or eggs, form in these two female sex organs. The ovaries also produce special hormones, called the sex hormones.

✳ HORMONES:
These are chemical substances produced by a number of organs in the body, such as the ovaries or the pituitary gland, which is located at the base of the brain. Hormones circulate in the blood and affect the way the body operates.

the male star

The male star of our story is the sperm. The sperm is the man's sex cell. Millions of sperm come off the "production line" inside the man's body every day. They're produced in the seminiferous tubules* that make up the testicles, the two ball-like organs that sit inside the sack of skin, or scrotum, that hangs under the penis. The sperm then move into the epididymis, a coiled tube that sits behind the testicles in the scrotum, where they stay until they're mature. When the man becomes sexually excited, for instance during sexual intercourse with a woman, the sperm exits the epididymis through a tube called the vas deferens, which takes it to the seminal vesicles. It's here, in the seminal vesicles, that millions of sperm are combined with a fluid called semen.* During an orgasm,* the semen and sperm combo is then shot out of the penis. This is ejaculation, when the sperm may finally find their way inside a woman's vagina and up to her uterus and fallopian tubes.

* SEMINIFEROUS TUBULES
These very thin tubes are balled up together to form the testicles. If laid end to end, they would measure up to 70 inches long. They empty into a long duct called the epididymis. The epididymis is the pathway that leads the sperm to the vas deferens, then they move to the seminal vesicles.

* SEMEN
Semen is a fluid made by the seminal vesicles. It nourishes the sperm and helps them move more easily.

* ORGASM
Touching or other stimulation of a man's penis or a woman's clitoris can result in this series of pleasurable muscular contractions. For men, orgasm results in ejaculation.

The Male Sex Organs

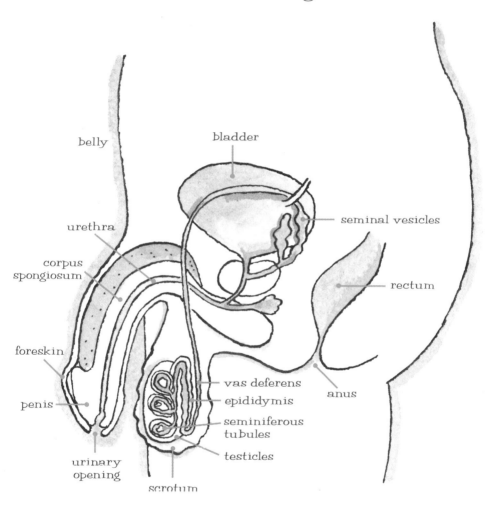

belly

bladder

seminal vesicles

urethra

corpus
spongiosum

rectum

foreskin

vas deferens

penis

epididymis

anus

seminiferous
tubules

urinary
opening

testicles

scrotum

cross section

Act 1
the meeting

Rewind for a moment: Imagine our stars, the ovum and the sperm, are each still offstage, the ovum in the fallopian tube and the sperm in the epididymis. But big things are about to happen. The woman, whose ovum is just waiting to meet a sperm, is lying in the arms of the man, whose sperm is just waiting to be ejaculated. The man and the woman love each other, so much, in fact, that they have decided to make a baby together, which means they are going to have intercourse. During this act, the man inserts his penis into the woman's vagina. And when the man ejaculates,

he releases about 300 million sperm into the woman's body.

These millions of cells find themselves propelled into the woman's vagina, near the entrance to the uterus. And there's a really mad rush to get in! Nature has thought of everything, though. The sperm have long tails, called

flagella, that enable them to travel very quickly. They swim into the uterus as fast as they can with one single purpose: to meet up with the ovum waiting in one of the fallopian tubes above. It's a true marathon, but on a tiny scale: they must travel six to seven inches at a speed of up to one inch per minute. That might not seem too fast, but when you consider that each sperm is so tiny that you'd need to magnify it to 400 times its normal size to even be able to see it, you get a better idea of just what quick and determined swimmers they are. Millions of sperm become exhausted and eventually drop out of the race. Others wander off course and die. The last remaining sperm that have located the entrance to the fallopian tube must reach the ovum soon, because the egg won't survive for more than twenty-four hours, even though the sperm can keep swimming for between three and five days.

The sperm that are still fighting to climb the fallopian tube finally find themselves "nose to nose" with a much bigger cell, the ovum! Does that mean the race is nearly won? Not yet—of all the squirming sperm that surround the much-desired ovum, only a single one can break through and fertilize it. But wait! One sperm has made it! It enters the ovum, which allows one, and only one, sperm inside. This moment is called conception or fertilization. The other sperm are out of luck. They will soon die off.

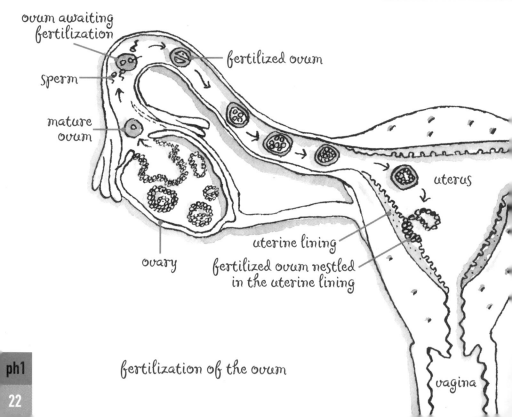

ovum awaiting fertilization

sperm

mature ovum

fertilized ovum

ovary

uterine lining

fertilized ovum nestled in the uterine lining

uterus

vagina

fertilization of the ovum

fertilization

The ovum and the sperm have joined forces to become one fertilized egg. The nucleus that was located at the center of the sperm has merged with the nucleus of the ovum. In other words, the two nuclei have combined. In three to four days, the fertilized egg will enter the uterus and become fastened to one of its walls.

In the uterus a small cozy nest awaits: the uterine lining, which has developed to be able to receive and nourish the fertilized egg. It has thickened and become swollen with blood, thanks to its many blood vessels. Here the safely sheltered egg can grow and become a beautiful baby in just nine months.

Sometimes, though, the planned encounter between ovum and sperm does not happen. Many different things can go wrong: the ovaries may not release an egg as expected or there could be too few sperm or sperm that are not fast enough to get to the ovum before it dies. In these cases, the couple is said to be infertile. But today, doctors can help couples who have fertility problems that prevent them from conceiving a baby. If it is the woman who is infertile, a common solution is in-vitro fertilization. Since the ovum and sperm cannot seem to meet on their own, a doctor will "arrange" this meeting in a test tube. First, the doctor takes a few mature ova from the woman's ovary. Then, she asks the man to give her some semen that contains sperm. Finally, she combines the sperm and the ova in a glass tube, where fertilization can take place. The fertilized eggs that come from this meeting are then put inside the woman's uterus. If all goes well, one or more of them will latch onto the uterine lining, and the woman will become pregnant.

If, on the other hand, it's the man who is infertile and there are not enough of his sperm or the sperm he does have are abnormal, the couple may resort to artificial insemination. In this case, the physician will use the sperm of another man to fertilize one of the woman's ova. She must get them from a sperm bank, an office where men go to donate their sperm to other men with fertility problems (or to women without male partners). Since the woman is ovulating normally, the physician will inject the donor's sperm into her vagina so that fertilization will occur just like it would in nature.

surrogacy & adoption

Sometimes, even in-vitro fertilization and artificial insemination don't work for the couple. When that happens, a woman may ask another woman to carry a baby for her in her uterus. These other women are called surrogate mothers. They either undergo artificial insemination with the man's sperm to become pregnant, or they use in-vitro fertilization to become pregnant with the couple's fertilized egg. The surrogate mother carries the couple's baby for nine months, and when it's born, she gives it to the infertile couple. This is a very big thing for the surrogate mother to do: it may be hard for her to give up the little person that's been growing inside of her for so long. In the past, there have been court cases in which the surrogate mother and the infertile couple have fought over who should get to raise the child. But there have been many surrogate mothers who have made the difficult decision to give up the child and been glad to help a couple become a family.

Instead of going through all this, a couple may decide to adopt a child instead. This means that a woman who is pregnant and feels she's not ready or able to bring up the baby herself chooses to give her child to a couple who is very much ready and able. This can happen as a closed adoption, where the couple and the child may never meet the birth mother, or an open adoption. In an open adoption, the couple may meet the pregnant mother during the pregnancy, be present at the birth, and allow the birth mother and the baby to know each other and even write letters or visit at times throughout the child's life. There is no right or wrong way to do it. Some people think that it would be too confusing for the child to know two different people as its mother. Others think that it's better if the child is given the chance to know where he or she came from, and believe that a child of a closed adoption may one day want to find his or her birth mother anyway.

Now back to our fertilized egg that has lodged itself in the uterus. No matter what method has been used to make it, its purpose is to develop into a human being. It needs about thirty-nine weeks, or a little more than nine months, to take shape and grow.

Once the egg is fertilized by the sperm, the two together are considered one cell. This cell then divides to make two cells. Next, these two cells divide again, making four, and so on—at this point, the cluster of cells is called an embryo. It begins to look a little like a bean with four small

nine months

1 month:

The embryo is less than 1 inch long. Its heart is already beating.

2 months:

The embryo weighs about 1 ounce and is between 1 and 1.5 inches long. The stomach, the intestines, and the urinary tract are being formed. The fingers and toes appear, and the eyes are visible on the face.

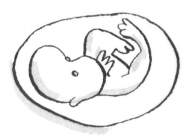

bumps that will later grow into two arms and two legs. The spinal column is pretty well formed already, but not the head. The embryo is floating in a bath of what is called amniotic fluid, which protects it from germs and from getting bumped around as its mother moves. It gets its food from the placenta, a flattened organ that looks a little like a pancake stuck to the wall of the uterus, which grows along with the embryo. The embryo is connected to the placenta by the umbilical cord. As the months pass, the embryo will start to look more and more like a baby.

until birth

3 months:

The embryo, which is nearly 5 inches long and weighs 2 ounces, looks like a human. It has become a fetus. Its face and limbs are clearly visible. The genital organs are developed.

4 months:

The fetus is nearly 8 inches long and weighs 8 ounces. It's moving around more. Its mother can feel it turning somersaults. It can even suck its thumb.

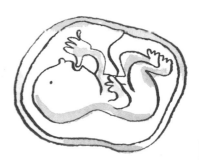

5 months:

The fetus is nearly 12 inches long and weighs 21 ounces. Its brain will grow by another 3 ounces each month.

6 months:

The fetus, now about 14.5 inches long, weighs a little more than 2 pounds. Its face is now very clearly defined: the eyebrows can be seen, the nose has its distinctive outline, and the neck can be clearly traced. It may even get the hiccups.

7 months:

The fetus weighs at least 3 pounds and is about 16.5 inches long. You can see it move from the outside; the smallest of its movements sends ripples to the surface of the mother's belly. At this point, the fetus hears outside noises. At birth, it will be able to recognize the voices of its parents.

8 months:

Since it weighs about 5.5 pounds and is about 18.5 inches long, the fetus is nearly ready to come out into the world. It changes positions, the head at the bottom, so that it can leave its mother's belly.

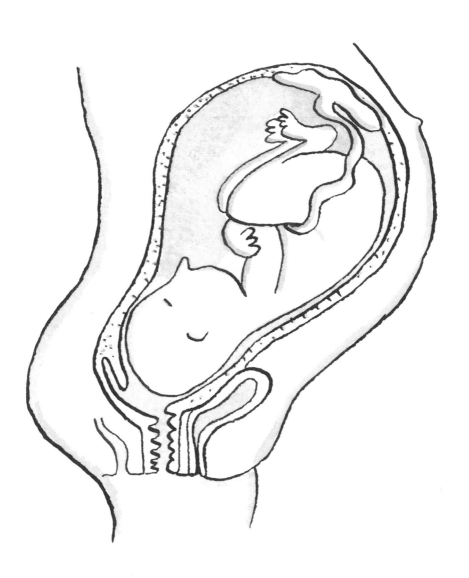

9 months:

The fetus weighs an average of 6.5 pounds and is nearly 20 inches long. It is living in cramped quarters inside its mother's belly. It's time for it to see the world and to show its little face to its parents!

the first baby pictures

Of course, all of these stages take place in the dark secrecy of the mother's uterus. The only way to view the developing baby is to use a sonogram, a device that lets you see a picture of the baby inside the uterus on a screen. The mother will typically have two or more sonograms during her pregnancy. They allow the doctor to see that the pregnancy is progressing normally and that the baby is healthy.

Other examinations are also performed to check the safety of the mother and her fetus. These include blood analyses and blood pressure tests. In some cases, the doctor may perform amniocentesis. In amniocentesis, a sample of amniotic fluid is taken from the mother's uterus. Analysis of the fluid will tell if the baby has genetic diseases, such as Down's syndrome or cystic fibrosis. Down's syndrome hinders normal development of the child. For example, he or she will have trouble talking and doing everyday tasks, such as dressing or eating. Cystic fibrosis affects the lungs. Our bodies normally produce mucus to grab and hold onto dust and germs in the lungs. In people who have cystic fibrosis, the body produces too much mucus and it fills up the lungs, making it difficult to breathe. Running tests during the mother's pregnancy helps catch these diseases early on so that doctors and parents have time to prepare for caring for a child with special needs.

d-day

We're getting close to the end of the story that started eight months and three weeks ago. The baby's doing fine, and so is the mother. The big day approaches. The baby now has only one hurdle left: to leave its mother's womb. To help it along, the mother's body has been getting ready. The bones in her pelvis have softened. Don't worry, though—they haven't become mushy like chewing gum. They've just become more flexible, so that the pelvis can expand as the baby passes through. When the mother goes into labor, her body will experience more changes: it works hard so the baby can be born. (That's why they call it labor!) First, she begins feeling contractions: This means that the walls of her uterus stiffen and then relax at regular intervals. When the contractions become very regular, very frequent, and, unfortunately, fairly painful, the mother and the doctors know that birth is about to happen. Around this time, the mother's water breaks, which means that the amniotic fluid that the baby was floating in has been released. The contractions break open the pouch that was holding in the fluid, which then flows out through the vagina.

birth

Thanks to the contractions, the cervix, which had been closed tight during the entire pregnancy, opens up little by little so that the baby can leave the uterus. This process lasts for several hours, usually time enough for the mother to reach the hospital maternity ward and get settled into a special room, or for a midwife to arrive at the mother's house, if the baby will be born at home. A doctor or midwife will help the mother give birth.

When the cervix has opened completely, the baby begins to leave the uterus head first. Each contraction then helps to slide the baby's body into the vagina. The mother pushes and clenches her muscles to help her baby move forward. The father coaches her along, providing moral support. Finally, the baby's head pokes through the entrance to

the vagina. The doctor or midwife then helps pull the child completely from the mother's body.

And there she is! The baby is crying, breathing air for the first time in her life! The doctor cuts the umbilical cord that connected the baby to the placenta (which doesn't hurt the baby or the mother at all). The baby is washed and weighed, then she is checked to make sure she's in perfect health. After that, of course, she is handed over to her mother and father. She may even get her first meal of milk from her mother's breast. This baby is unique. Whether a girl or a boy, this child is identical to no other baby on earth. The baby will grow every day. It will become a woman or a man...who will have sexual intercourse...and maybe a baby of his or her own. This is how life carries on.

phase

2

everything you
always
wanted to know...
but were
not about to ask

YOUR

I've got hair. Is that normal?

HELP! THEY'RE
GROWING!

mirror, mirror..

IS IT SERIOUS, DOC?

GROWING BODY

becoming
a woman

My pimples are actually bigger than my breasts!

When you were little, you had to be forced to take baths. But now you spend hours in the bathroom grooming and looking at your new body in the mirror—and you're not sure if you like what you see. Maybe your breasts have grown so much that you hide them under sweaters. Or maybe you think they haven't grown enough, compared to all your friends'. You ask yourself a thousand and one questions: "Why hasn't my period started?" "What is this clear liquid that's flowing from my vagina?" "Why is my left breast bigger than my right one?" "Am I normal?"

Never doubt it for a second: you're completely normal. The changes in your body are going to take place over several years, and they happen at a slightly different time and pace for every girl. So there's no need to panic if your breasts don't start to grow when you're eleven or if your period hasn't started when you're thirteen. There is no hard and fast rule as to when these things will take place. And because each girl is unique and different, the information we're about to give is just a guideline—these events might happen a little sooner or a little later for you, and you'd still be totally normal.

As a general rule, girls' bodies start to change at the age of nine or ten. That's when puberty begins. The body starts making new hormones, or chemical substances, that affect the different parts of the body. Girls figures change gradually. The pelvis gets bigger. Breasts appear. The pubis, the part of the body above the vagina, becomes covered with hair. Between ages twelve and fourteen, the first period arrives. That means that each month from then on, menstrual blood will flow out of the vagina for about five days. Finally, hair starts to grow on the underarms.

Do you want to know more? Here are answers to the questions that you may be asking yourself:

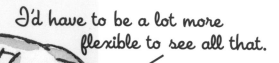

I'd have to be a lot more flexible to see all that.

Where exactly are my sex organs?

You have both internal (inner) and external (outer) sex organs. The outer ones are located below the pubis and between the thighs, and they make up the vulva. The vulva has "lips," called the labia majora, which are located alongside smaller lips called the labia minora. These two pairs of lips surround the entrance to the vagina. The labia minora look like small bulges of flesh, and their size varies from one woman to another. The clitoris, a small, extremely sensitive organ, is found in front of these labia minora. It is stimulation of the clitoris that can cause an orgasm, a pleasurable contraction of muscles.

The opening through which you urinate is located below the clitoris. The entrance to the vagina is a little lower down from that. The vagina, the uterus, both fallopian tubes, and the two ovaries make up your inner sex organs. The vagina is a muscular hollow tube measuring about three to six inches long leading to the cervix, an opening into the uterus. The uterus is a muscular hollow organ that shelters the fertilized ovum, embryo, and fetus during pregnancy. The fallopian tubes connect the uterus to the ovaries, where ova grow.

What are periods?

Every month or so, beginning in puberty, menstrual blood will flow from your vagina for three to seven days. This bleeding is absolutely normal, and it doesn't hurt at all. This will happen until you're around fifty, and then it will stop.

This blood comes from the mucus membrane that lines the inside of your uterus. Each month one ovum, or egg, matures, slips out of an ovary, and is collected by one of the fallopian tubes. It slowly makes its way down the fallopian tube toward the uterus. At this point, if you were to have sex with a man and he ejaculated, the ovum might be fertilized by one of his sperm. If that happens, the fertilized ovum continues to move down into the uterus and attaches itself to the wall—more precisely, to the mucus membrane that has been thickening with blood so that it can nourish a fertilized egg. But if the ovum is not fertilized by a sperm, it dies. Since there's no fertilized egg, the blood that has made the uterus's walls swell up is useless. So the body gets rid of it. The unneeded blood flows out of the uterus through the vagina and outside the woman's body. It takes a period of about three to seven days for it all to come out, and that period is called ...a period!

Usually, twenty-eight days pass between the first day of your period and the start of the next. This span of time is called the menstrual cycle. It varies slightly for every woman, so your cycle might be shorter (say, twenty-six days) or longer (thirty to thirty-two days).

I've got my period! ⎯⎯⎯

When a woman reaches fifty to fifty-five years of age, the menstrual cycle stops. At this point, the woman can no longer ovulate, that is, release mature ova. She can no longer have children. The mucus membrane of her uterus no longer has to swell up with blood so that it can take care of a fertilized ovum. Therefore, she doesn't get her period anymore. This is called menopause.

Can I lose too much blood during my period?

It can seem as if a lot of blood is flowing out during your period, but it's actually just four to six tablespoons' worth. And you only lose the blood that was in the lining of your uterus. The uterus is not connected to the other organs (intestines, stomach, bladder, etc.) in your belly, so there's no danger of blood from other places draining out during your period. It's all a perfect system.

Look, I'm having my period, I'm menstruating, Aunt Flo is visiting, my little friend is here, I'm on the rag, I'm surfing the crimson tide, I'm riding the cotton pony, in short, it's Niagara Falls ... get it? Or do you want me to draw you a picture, too?

I think I see...

Exercise helps cramps.

What if I don't get my period every month?

Your period may not be regular for the first two years, or even longer. So you may get your period later or sooner than you expect it each month as your body gets used to its new functions. But if your period stops for two months, see your family doctor or a gynecologist just to make sure that there's nothing wrong, or, if you are sexually active, that you are not pregnant.

Can I use a tampon from the time I have my first period?

A tampon is a small tube-shaped piece of cotton that you insert into the vagina. When the menstrual blood flows out of the uterus, the tampon swells and forms a sort of plug that prevents the blood from coming out into your underwear. You can use a tampon during your first period without any worries, but it might take a couple tries to get it in there comfortably. Buy the smallest ones available when you first start out, the ones marked "slender" or "junior absorbency." If you can't place a tampon in the right position (you'll know because it will feel uncomfortable), or just don't like the idea of them yet, you may want to use a sanitary napkin, or pad. These are fairly thick protective pads that stick inside your underwear and catch the blood as it comes out. To avoid infection, remember to change your pad or tampon at least every four to eight hours, or sooner if it fills up with blood before then.

I'm PMSing big time . . .

Am I still a virgin if I use tampons?

To be a virgin means that you have never had sexual intercourse. Inserting a tampon inside your vagina has nothing to do with virginity. You will be a virgin until the time you first have sex.

I'm fifteen and still haven't gotten my period. Am I normal?

By the age of fifteen, if your body shows no signs of puberty, that is, if your breasts or body hair are not growing, this may be an indication of an abnormal delay. If this happens, go see your family doctor or a gynecologist. But if everything else is going according to schedule, wait patiently for your period. It'll come before long!

I feel awful before my period. Is that normal?

A lot of women experience PMS, or premenstrual syndrome, during which they feel bloated, have headaches, or just generally don't feel great. Drinking water and getting exercise can help.

And menstruation itself can bring cramps that come from slight contractions of the uterus. Try a heating pad, stretching, or a pain reliever like ibuprofin. If that doesn't work and you feel like the pain is really strong, see your doctor to make sure there's nothing wrong.

I don't even feel it when I have my period . . .

How do I know I can have children?

Lots of girls ask themselves this question, even if they've never said the words out loud. But it's absolutely not something you have to worry about. The start of your period suggests that your body is working normally. The only way you'll know for sure is if you become pregnant, and you certainly don't want that to happen just yet. You've got plenty of time before you even have to start thinking about this.

What's this whitish fluid that comes out into my underwear when I don't have my period?

This small amount of colorless or whitish fluid coming from your vagina is called discharge. It might look a little like egg whites, or like mucus. In fact, its official name is cervical mucus. Some women produce a lot, some produce a little, but either way it's totally normal. This mucus is secreted by the cervix and flows little by little into the vagina. It's there to make penetration and intercourse easier, and to help sperm move forward through the vagina and the uterus toward the ovum.

I'm really starting to look like an adult . . .

How do breasts develop?

Breasts grow under the influence of hormones, those chemical substances that the body produces. Gradually, the tissues that make up the breasts get larger. Simultaneously, the areola, the colored area surrounding the nipple, becomes larger and may get lighter or darker in color. The breasts start to take shape. It normally takes about two to four years for them to reach their final size.

Will they be big or small?

That depends a lot on your family genes. If all of your female relatives have small breasts, it would be surprising if yours were big—and vice versa—although it can happen. Rest assured, though, there isn't just one size that's most attractive. There are beautiful women with small breasts and beautiful women with large breasts. And as for men, they seem to appreciate all types. But if a boy ever makes a rude remark about your breasts, you can safely put him in the "immature jerk" category.

Is it normal to have one breast that's bigger than the other?

Absolutely—it's very common. Our bodies are not perfectly symmetrical, so most women find that one breast is slightly larger than the other. But usually it's only the owner of the breasts who can tell!

When should I wear a bra?

Breasts are not muscles, so they have no natural support. They are made up of fatty tissue that contains the glands that will produce milk after the birth of a baby. Over time, breasts may droop a little, especially larger ones. That's why women wear bras (well, that and because they make our clothes look better!). You can start wearing a bra whenever you feel that it will make you more comfortable. A bra is especially helpful if you play a sport that makes your breasts bounce around a lot.

becoming
a m a n

the penis

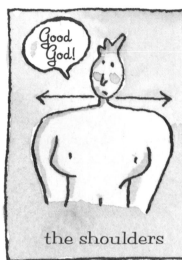

the shoulders

Don't freak out if your best friend now towers over you by a full head. Or if he swears that his penis has gotten bigger, while yours doesn't seem to have grown a bit. You're still normal. Everyone's body changes, but not necessarily at the same time. Puberty, the transition stage from childhood to maturity, may start earlier in some boys, and later in others.

Generally speaking, boys see the first signs of puberty at about twelve or thirteen. Just as with girls, hormones are the substances that spur changes in the male body. First off, the testicles get bigger. And the scrotum, the skin sack that surrounds the two testicles, matures, thickens, and gets a wrinkled look. It may also become redder or browner. The first hairs spring up on the pubis, the areas above the penis, and also on the abdomen, chest, and the under arms. The penis lengthens

mpits   the beard   the voice

and thickens. Hair starts to grow on the chin and will later turn into a beard. Muscles pump up over the entire body, and the shoulders become broader than the hips. Finally, your voice changes, or breaks. This process lasts for a few months, and can be a little embarrassing at times. The little boy's voice you've had your whole life up till now will suddenly warble as it tries to get out a sentence, switching abruptly from shrill high tones to the emerging bass notes. It doesn't sound very cool, and doesn't seem to go with your new masculine physique, but at least it's happening to most of the other guys, too.

Other changes may trouble you as well, things you can't bring yourself to talk about openly to your parents or even your friends. Here are some of the biggest questions along with a few simple answers:

What's an erection?

When your penis, which is usually soft and tends to droop, suddenly hardens and jumps to attention, that's an erection. It's actually a rush of blood that causes the penis to become erect. The penis is not a muscle, nor does it have any bones. It's made up of tissues capable of absorbing and holding blood. These tissues have a springy quality, making the inner parts of your penis a little like a sponge. When blood flows into it, the penis swells up just like a waterlogged sponge. And when the blood recedes, the penis gets smaller again, returning to its "at ease" position. And that's the end of that erection.

What causes this surge of blood to the penis?

Sexual desire, stimulation from outside, and sleep can spark an erection.

sexual desire

Let's say you're in love with a girl. When you see her, when you hold her hand or kiss her, your penis swells and you're having an erection. The feelings of physical attraction you're having cause your erection. You feel like holding her in your arms, kissing her, touching her body. It's this desire that springs your penis into action. You can also cause an erection when you have fantasies. That is, when you imagine situations in which you're experiencing sexual desire. Erotic, or sexual, dreams can also produce an erection.

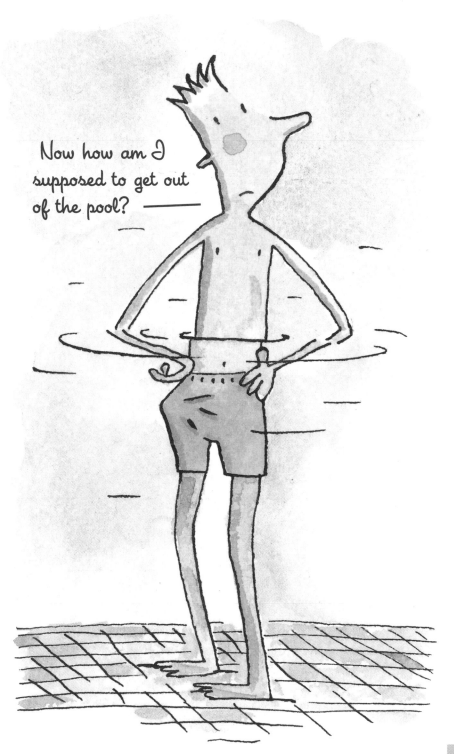

outside stimulation

Some sports activities may trigger an erection, even though you don't want one at that particular moment. Climbing a rope or riding a horse may lead to an erection when your penis rubs against the rope or saddle. The same thing happens when you stroke your penis, since, again, rubbing will arouse it.

sleep

During a specific phase of sleep, called REM sleep, the brain is hard at work. Your whole body is in a highly reactive state, which causes invol-

untary movements of your body parts, including the penis. This explains why men often wake up with an erection, and why, in fact, most men experience three or four erections every night. All of this is completely normal, so don't be embarrassed if an erection sneaks up on you, either in broad daylight or in the privacy of your bedroom.

Can you explain what an ejaculation is?

Ejaculation means the forceful release of semen, which contains sperm, from the penis. Ejaculation can take place only after you have an erection. In other words, ejaculation can never happen while the penis is simply resting comfortably. During sexual intercourse, ejaculation marks the beginning of the sperms' attempts to fertilize an egg, and happens at the exact moment when the man feels the most intense pleasure.

But your first ejaculation will likely come at night, while you're asleep. It's called a "wet dream." This first ejaculation is important, it's a milestone in your emerging sexuality. However, you might not feel it's necessary to report this big milestone to your whole family. Girls often feel just as shy about telling their families that they've had their first period. Even though these things are normal, natural, and happen to every man and woman, for some reason it's still embarrassing to talk about them out loud, especially during polite dinner conversation. But if you sense that your parents, and particularly your father, are ready to talk about these things, don't hesitate to broach the subject. This is a major event, after all, and you'll go through it thousands of times during your life. There is nothing dirty or shameful about it.

At what age do boys start to ejaculate?

The first ejaculations typically occur at between twelve and thirteen years of age. What's true about girls and periods also applies here: there is no firm and fast rule. The first ejaculation will arrive sooner or later.

Can you urinate and ejaculate at the same time?

Boys often imagine that urine and sperm are going to get mixed up together. Actually, the penis has a small muscle inside (the sphincter) that shuts off the urethra when erection and ejaculation are taking place. That means that you couldn't possibly ever urinate and ejaculate at the same time.

What happens to the sperm if I don't ejaculate?

There's no chance that your testicles will swell from built up sperm just because you haven't ejaculated for a long time. The testicles manufacture

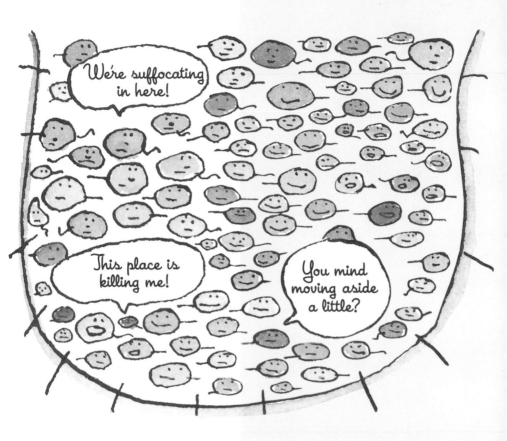

the sperm, but don't store them. When the sperm are ready to go through the final maturation process, they're sent to the epididymus. They're getting ready for the moment when they will be ejected during ejaculation. But if you do not, in fact, ejaculate for several weeks or months, specific cells, called macrophages, destroy the stored sperm. The process then repeats itself: new sperm are produced and stored in the epididymus until they are ejaculated or destroyed.

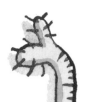

Will my penis be long enough?

You should learn this now once and for all: penises come in all sizes. They may also have different shapes. Generally speaking, an erect penis is longer and has more volume than a penis in its resting state. No matter the size and shape, however, the ability to make love and give pleasure has nothing—seriously, nothing—to do with length. So don't get a complex over your size. Women don't go around holding up rulers to measure their partners' penises.

I was circumcised. Can that create problems when I make love?

Circumcision is a minor surgical operation performed on infants during which the fold of skin covering the glans penis, that is, the rounded head of the penis, is removed. This fold of skin is called the foreskin. Circumcision is a cultural norm in some places and appears to have some hygiene benefits. But it's also done for religious purposes. In the Jewish and Muslim faiths, circumcision is celebrated as a ritual.

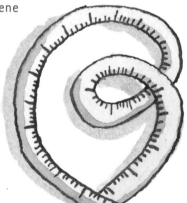

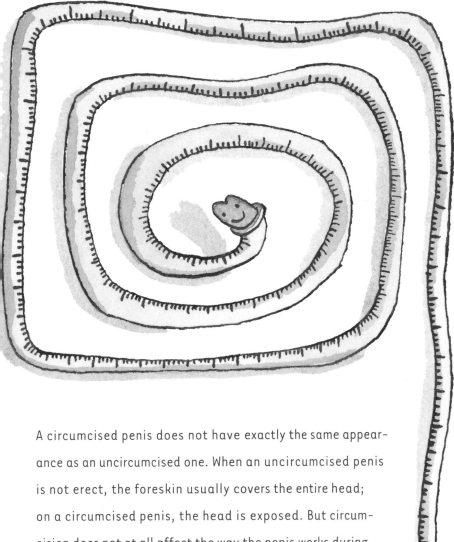

A circumcised penis does not have exactly the same appearance as an uncircumcised one. When an uncircumcised penis is not erect, the foreskin usually covers the entire head; on a circumcised penis, the head is exposed. But circumcision does not at all affect the way the penis works during erection and ejaculation. Whether you're circumcised or not, you'll have sex the same way as any other man.

Why are the testicles on the outside of the body?

Sperm are particular: they can be made only when the temperature is about 91.5°F. But since our body temperature is 98.6°F, it's too hot inside to manufacture them. Hanging outside the main part of the body, the testicles can take advantage of cooler weather!

My nipples have gotten bigger. Is this normal?

It's true: boys' nipples grow bigger during puberty and become more sensitive. This development is entirely normal, and the production of sexual hormones is at the root of it all. After a few months, though, they go back to the way they were before. (If they don't, you might want to talk to your doctor about it.)

I'm fifteen and I still look like a kid. Is this normal?

For many boys, puberty comes later than they'd prefer. At fourteen or fifteen they still look like little boys, while their friends have grown bigger and more muscular as they advance toward adulthood. If you are one of these late bloomers, don't worry too much: your body will pass through these changes, only a little later, perhaps between the ages of fifteen and sixteen. If the delay is weighing on your mind, talk to your doctor and he can provide all the reassurance you need.

taming your
new body

You have now learned about the many changes going on in the inside and outside of your body. This new knowledge probably won't stop you from scrutinizing yourself for hours at a time in front of the bathroom mirror. That's okay. Who cares if the whole family is banging on the door outside, waiting for their turn to get in! This self-observation is an excellent way to get used to your new appearance. At the same time, though, you shouldn't be too hard on yourself. The extra hair, the extra weight—these are things that everyone has. You're your own worst critic, and the parts about your new self that you may not

This shirt looks even better than it did last year!

like yet are most likely things that nobody but you notices. Instead of criticizing yourself, focus on the positive changes to your body, the way your new breasts or your broad chest fill out a T-shirt in a way they never did before. Becoming an adult is a good thing, not something you need to be self-conscious about.

However you feel about your new body, the most important thing is that you treat it well. Crash dieting to get rid of your softer hips or to make your weight class in wrestling can do serious harm. You need nourishment to grow and change.

Another way to take good care of yourself is to wash regularly. Once puberty comes, you begin to sweat more, so you'll want to shower often, especially after exercising. (Girls: You can and should bathe just like normal when you have your period.) You'll probably also want to start using an underarm antiperspirant or deodorant.

One drawback to adolescence for both boys and girls is acne. Pimples, whiteheads, and blackheads may pop up, and not only on your face, but your back, chest, and even your buttocks. This major annoyance is the result of the excess sebum produced during puberty. Sebum is a substance manufactured by the skin. When there is too much of it, it clogs the pores, those minuscule holes that let the skin release sweat. This makes pimples begin to sprout. But drugstore shelves are full of products designed to help cleanse your skin and treat your acne. If you have a severe case that doesn't respond to any of these treatments, consult a dermatologist, who can prescribe a more effective remedy.

the doctor is in

While a dermatologist can help you deal with your acne, don't forget about your family doctor or pediatrician. She can answer all the questions you have about your development and help with your ailments or worries. Ideally, you'll build a trusting relationship with her in which you feel comfortable enough to tell her what's bothering you. After all, that's what she's there for. You can even ask specifically that everything you tell her be kept just between the two of you and not shared with your mom or dad. From this time on, your parents must learn to respect your private life.

To doctors, every question is an important one. They understand that you want to know what's happening to you. Girls should start seeing a gynecologist either by age eighteen or when they have intercourse for the first time, whichever comes first. You can choose either a male or female doctor, depending on whom you feel more comfortable with. You have the right to consult with him or her confidentially, since gynecologists, too, must abide by the principle of medical privacy. But if you're worried, you might choose to see a different doctor than your mom or other family members see, so there's no connection at all. One way to do this is to visit a local family planning clinic, like Planned Parenthood. They serve both men and women, and the services are usually free of charge. A gynecologist can prescribe contraceptive methods, such as the pill, to prevent pregnancy. She also performs a pelvic exam to make sure you're completely healthy. And when you have children, she'll monitor the progress of your pregnancy. Making an appointment with a gynecologist once a year is a good habit to get into.

falling in love

SEXUAL

SOUND BODY, SOUND MIND

PROTECTING YOURSELF

to each his own

the heat of the moment

INTERCOURSE

pleasure and DISPLEASURE

love's myste

Not so long ago, open-mouth kissing and love scenes in movies made you squirm (especially when watching them with your parents!). But now, here you are, fascinated by what can happen between two people who love each other. You may have seen magazines photos or movies showing people making love. If anything, they prove that sex does in fact usually involve a man inserting his penis into a woman's vagina. But lots of times movies and magazines make the whole thing look more like exercise than romance. Seeing those kinds of images, you might wonder what's so special and magical about sex? The way movie couples do it, sex can look more like two sweaty people bumping back and forth against each other—not very romantic!

The truth is that sexual intercourse can be many things. If you believe

Blah, Blah, Blah   Smack, Smack   ah! a

ries

only what medical diagrams or movies show sex to be, you don't get the full picture. On the other hand, if you understand that intercourse can be the culminating act of a loving relationship with another person, the picture suddenly looks a lot warmer, a lot more wonderful. When two people care about each other, making love becomes a shared act of intimacy and tenderness. What had seemed just mechanical emerges as truly romantic. By exchanging kisses and caresses, by joining their bodies, the two partners show their feelings and their desire to give and receive pleasure. The expression "sexual relations" reveals its full meaning: the existence of a strong relationship that inspires two people to share their most private possessions—their bodies and their sexuality.

intercourse

Two people meeting for the first time don't simply fall into bed and make love just because they find each other attractive. Before that happens, they have to get know each other. Little by little, as they grow closer, they exchange more intimate gestures of tenderness— kisses and caresses. Only after they have been with each other for a certain period will they make the choice to deepen the relationship even further by making love, or in other words, having sex.

Like we've said before, sex isn't just about intercourse. Penetration doesn't just happen at the sound of the starting gun, as in: "Ready, undress, go!" There's a lot of kissing and touching and caressing that goes on before the couple is reading to have actual intercourse. Both of them need a warming up period while their bodies and their minds get truly prepared to make love. Rushing the act makes it much less pleasurable. In other words, they need time.

This concept of time is an important one. Before you ever have intercourse, you'll need time to go through the steps, one by one, that will lead you from your first kiss to your "first time." You won't necessarily pass through all of the steps with the first person you have a relationship with. Even though you may have already kissed a boy or girl, and even though your body has developed and you feel like an adult,

this doesn't automatically mean that you're ready to have intercourse, because in matters of love, the body is not enough. Your mind and your heart have to be ready, too. Before they are, your emotions might feel muddled and confused. You know you feel strongly for someone, and you're doing everything in your power to get him or her to like you back. But is it really love, or just physical attraction, or what? There's no easy answer to these kinds of questions. It's not an easy job, sorting out all of these longings, these desires, these feelings rumbling around in your head and knocking against each other. But don't worry—this uncertainty won't last forever. As the months and years pass, you'll get to know yourself better and better, and you'll start to understand your own feelings more easily and recognize what they mean. And soon enough, you'll know when, in the natural course of your life, you're ready to have your first sexual experience.

the first time

Does it hurt?

Even though you might not be ready for sex yet, you're probably really curious about what the first time is like. How does it happen? What does it feel like? Girls often worry that penetration will be painful. Boys, on the other hand, worry that they won't be able to perform, that they'll be too nervous to get an erection. Young people have been having these same concerns for centuries. While you know in your head how intercourse happens, it still seems completely intimidating before you've done it. You don't really want to ask your parents what it's like, since hearing them recount their own sexual exploits isn't exactly top on your list of fun things to do. And it can be just as hard to talk about this stuff with your more experienced friends because of the fear

At this point, I'd do it with just about anybody!

that they'll make fun of you. If you ever talk to someone who boasts that they've "done it," you know that they never really tell the whole story, and can't really explain the feelings they felt during it. The first time is a unique experience that can be talked about, but can't really be fully shared with someone else. That said, before you decide to have this experience for yourself, bear in mind these few pieces of advice:

Never tell yourself: "I have to have sex by the time I'm eighteen (or twenty-one, or whenever)." You're not in a competition with your friends. There's no prize for the fastest. So don't let yourself be influenced by the people you hang around with. You want to have sex not to be like your friends, but because you are in love with another person and are ready to share your heart and your body with him or her. That may happen for you when you're 17, 20, or 25. It's your life, and it concerns only you.

You shouldn't let your boyfriend or girlfriend push you into something you're not ready for. Just because having sex might be the right decision for your partner, it doesn't mean it's right for you. Even if you're in a loving relationship, the choice is still yours and yours alone. And if the person who supposedly loves you is willing to break up with you because you're not ready, that's just confirmation

Even if he doesn't come for ten years, I'll wait for Prince Charming.

that he or she wasn't the right person for you to have your first time with, anyway.

You may have a wonderful fantasy in your head of what your first time will be like. Not that you shouldn't hold onto that dream, but you might be better prepared by knowing that nine times out of ten, things won't go exactly according to expectations. One of you will laugh when you think you're not supposed to, funny bodily noises will be made, and other little things you can't foresee will most likely happen. Having a sense of humor is the best way to deal with this stuff. Both you and your partner will be anxious, nervous, and excited, all the while trying to make the whole event go smoothly and naturally, like you do this kind of thing every day. But if you've been honest with your partner and he or she knows that this is your first time, you can relax. You're not expected to be an expert from day one. A good boyfriend or girlfriend will be understanding, attentive, and tender, and won't think less of you if everything doesn't go perfectly.

You know, it's my first time.

Having intercourse for the first time is not always a life-altering experience. It might even be a little disappointing. Girls—it might take some time and exploration before sex becomes truly pleasurable. Boys—it's not uncommon to ejaculate sooner than you'd like. The emotions you'll be feeling will be intense, and make it difficult to control the timing of these things. But again, this happens to almost everyone. Your sex life is just beginning, and your experiences will only get better with time.

Well, you've got to start somewhere!

When you know that you're ready to have intercourse with the person you love, you must use protection. Condoms are the best way to prevent sexually-transmitted diseases and are also very effective against pregnancy. (Find out more about condoms and birth control methods on pages 86–91.) Get to know these little rubber hats before your first sexual experience. It's important for both boys and girls to know how to use them— that way, even if one of you doesn't know how to do it correctly, the other will. Boys can practice on themselves in the privacy of their rooms, and girls can actually use bananas to get the hang of putting a condom on a penis! It's also important for girls as well as guys to take responsibility for buying or obtaining condoms. If your partner forgets, you'll still be protected. You may feel embarrassed when the store clerk rings up your purchase, but he's probably rung up hundreds of condom purchases and won't care a bit, and anyway, what's a little embarrassment compared to a painful disease or pregnancy!

desire &

As we've just said, the first experience does not usually involve complete, undeniable pleasure. It's logical to think that sharing a very passionate exchange with someone you're highly attracted to will feel incredible. And in time, it will. But while desire is something we're born with, the ability to give and receive pleasure is learned. As you become more experienced, you'll learn that certain types of caresses feel better to you than others—and they won't necessarily be the same ones your friends report liking. You'll also learn to recognize which kisses and touches your partner reacts to more strongly. It's this learning process that will allow you to enjoy intercourse, and to experience orgasm.

An orgasm is the "climax of sexual excitement." (That's actually what it says in Webster's dictionary.) It's when a person experiences the most intense moment of pleasure. Trying to describe in words a sensation that each human being experiences in his or her own way is difficult. Men have an orgasm each time they ejaculate. A woman's orgasm, on the other hand, doesn't coincide with something as obvious as ejaculation. Whether it's fair or not, most instances of sex end with the man having an orgasm, but women may not always have an orgasm every time they have intercourse, especially at first. But this will change as you get to know your own body and your partner's body.

pleasure

oral sex

There are other acts besides intercourse than can bring about orgasm in both men and women. One of these is oral sex, which is when one partner stimulates the genitals of the other with his or her tongue and mouth. Though

you're still a virgin until you've had intercourse, many people consider oral sex to be just as serious and intimate as intercourse. Others believe oral sex is not actual sex, but rather a less serious sexual act, or part of foreplay. Whatever you think it is, it does have similar potential consequences as intercourse. While you can't get pregnant from oral sex, you can get sexually transmitted diseases. So you need to protect yourself—that means guys should wear a condom and girls should cover their genitals with a dental dam (a small piece of latex made just for this purpose). Remember also that oral sex can carry the same emotional consequences as intercourse—with both of these sexual acts, you're sharing your body with another person, and that's a big step.

solo sex

You may have already discovered how to give yourself pleasure by masturbating—that is, by touching your genitals in a sexual way. Almost everyone has done it, even though hardly anyone talks about it. While some boys may admit to it among friends, most girls wouldn't do the same. Why? Masturbation is a totally natural, but highly personal act. For centuries, it was a taboo subject. The only time it was mentioned was when it was being condemned. While we know today that it is perfectly normal and healthy, some of the stigma attached to it has remained. But while it may not make a good casual conversation topic, many adults, both men and women, masturbated as adolescents, and

Hi, everyone! I know my body much better this morning!

many continue the practice during their entire life.

If you feel no urge to masturbate, that's fine—there's no use forcing yourself. Whether you do try it at some point or you don't, you shouldn't feel guilty about it. Do not listen to people who claim that it will zap your energy before a big game, or make you grow hair on your palms or go blind or whatever. There's no truth to any of this.

Masturbation is not another way of making love, and doesn't make you any less a virgin. That requires you to have sexual intercourse. Masturbation can, however, help you get to know your body better and discover new, very good sensations.

loving a person of the same sex

Sexual orientation refers to whether a person is attracted to people of the same sex or people of the opposite sex. Those who are attracted to the opposite sex are called heterosexual or straight, and those who are attracted to the same sex are called homosexual or gay (or lesbian, if the person is a woman). Today, your sexual orientation is believed to be something that you're born with—that is, you don't choose to be gay or straight, it's just something you've always felt inside. About 10 percent of men and women identify themselves as gay or lesbian.

While society has come a long way in accepting homosexuality, it's still a sensitive subject for some. In countries like Canada and the Netherlands, gay and lesbian couples can marry, but in the U.S. these marriages aren't legally recognized...yet! More and more Americans believe that same-sex couples should enjoy the same rights as straight ones.

As you get older, you may have feelings of attraction to a friend of the same sex. This may mean that you are gay or it may not. These kinds of feelings often happen within close friendships, since you're both discovering new bodies and new emotions. You may even experiment physically with him or her and still go on to have relationships with members of the opposite sex. However, if your attraction to people of the same sex continues throughout your teenage years, you will know that you are gay or lesbian. This realization can bring extra feelings of anxiety to an already difficult time in your life. One of the best ways to calm these anxieties is to talk to and get to know other gay and lesbian teenagers. The Gay, Lesbian & Straight Education Network (GLSEN) is a great resource. They have a list of the more than five hundred gay/straight alliance organizations at high schools across the country, and a terrific Web site with advice about coming out and information about hotlines, events, and even gay history. You can also read about bisexuality (being attracted to people of both sexes) and issues of gender identity. The address is www.glsen.org. Another good organization is PFLAG—Parents, Families and Friends of Lesbians and Gays. They can help you talk to your family and become comfortable with your emerging sexuality. Their Web site address is www.pflag.org. As with anything, it helps to get the facts and advice from people who have had similar experiences.

However you may feel about your sexual identity now, it is something that you can grow more comfortable and happy with in time. A gay friend says, "It took some time for me to understand who I was and that I was okay. My true friends saw me as me and that was all that mattered." In other words, it is good to be true to yourself and your feelings.

pregnancy

One day you will have sex, and sex carries with it certain potential—and sometimes unwanted—consequences. One of these is pregnancy. At some point in your life, the news that you're going to be a parent will be cause for celebration. But as a teenager, you probably don't have the money to raise a child, nor the time, what with school and homework and maybe college down the road. Most teens just aren't ready to handle the responsibility of caring for a baby.

Beginning the month or so before their first period, girls may become pregnant if they have intercourse. Similarly, boys can fertilize an egg as soon as they can ejaculate. That means that around the age of thirteen, a girl and a boy are capable of making a baby. Don't believe

I'm pregnant...

Calm down, we'll talk about it. I won't let you down.

the idea that you can't get pregnant just because it's your first time having intercourse. You'll need to use contraception the first time and every time.

The most obvious sign of pregnancy is a late period. You might also notice a feeling of nausea, especially in the mornings, and sore or tender breasts. To find out for sure if you're pregnant, you'll need to take an at-home pregnancy test (sold at drugstores) or visit your doctor or local clinic. Pregnancy tests, whether done yourself or by a physician, detect whether or not certain pregnancy hormones are present in your urine. If you are pregnant, you'll need to make a choice about what to do: have the baby and raise it, have the baby and give it up for adoption, or have an abortion (see page 92 for more info). Talking to your doctor and your family can be a big help in making this decision.

methods of
contraception

Contraception refers to the prevention of pregnancy. The purpose of contraception is to prevent fertilization of an ovum by a sperm and/or implantation of a fertilized ovum in the uterus. None of the following methods is 100 percent effective, but they come fairly close with proper use.

the pill.

Birth control pills contain hormones that make a woman's body think it's already pregnant, so it stops ovulating. In other words, they prevent ova from leaving the ovaries. When intercourse takes place, the sperm from the male reach the fallopian tubes, but there's no ovum there to fertilize.

The pill is an oral form of contraception, meaning you swallow it. To

The pill, what a stroke of genius!

make sure the pill is effective, you must remember to take it every day, preferably at about the same time every day. If you forget more than a couple of times, you won't be protected. So forgetful types might instead consider a birth control patch or injection, which work similarly to the pill. You need a prescription to get each of these, which means you must see a doctor. You should never borrow any of these from a friend or your mother!

You can take the pill for as long as you want without risk to your health. In fact, the pill can actually make your periods lighter, decrease cramps, and help clear up acne. However, it's important that you not smoke while you're on birth control pills, as this can lead to problems such as blood clots. And beware: as soon as you stop taking your pills, you can become pregnant again.

the morning-after pill.

The morning-after pill, also called emergency contraception, isn't something you want to use as your regular form of contraception. Women take these high-dose hormone pills up to three days after unprotected sex to prevent pregnancy. They prevent the lining of the uterus from forming, so that a fertilized ovum cannot be implanted in it. This, therefore, allows the fertilized egg to be expelled from the uterus. The morning-after pill is more expensive than regular birth control pills, and can cause nausea and stomach upset. It's really something that should be used only when other contraceptive methods have been accidentally forgotten or, say, when a condom breaks. You can get it at a family-planning clinic or by prescription from your doctor. You can even get it in advance, so that if an accident happens, it's there in your medicine cabinet when you need it.

I forgot!

the condom.

The condom is the only contraceptive method used on the male body. It is a very thin sheath of rubber that is unrolled over the penis to cover it during intercourse. The condom catches the sperm when the man ejaculates, preventing it from flowing into the woman's vagina. No sperm in the vagina means the ovum can't be fertilized and pregnancy can't take place. To work, it must be used correctly: If the condom is poorly placed on the penis, or if it tears, the sperm can escape. A new condom must be used for each act of intercourse: a condom can be used once, and only once.

You can buy condoms without a prescription in drugstores, super-markets, and at automatic dispensing machines found in some schools and restrooms. The most effective condoms are made of latex (in fact, these are the only kind that also prevent the spread of sexually transmitted diseases such as HIV and herpes), and have a small space, or reservoir, at the tip that prevents the condom from stretching too tight and tearing during ejaculation. For greater comfort, you should use lubricated condoms. These condoms are covered with a substance that makes penetration smoother and easier.

PUTTING ON THE CONDOM

tear the package carefully

put the condom on end of penis as though it were a little hat

← resevoir

① ② ③

squeeze the resevoir with one hand, unroll rest of condom with the other

④ ⑤

You're done!

(avoid using teeth or fingernails to open package or unroll condom)

other contraceptive methods

There are several other ways to help prevent pregnancy that aren't quite as appropriate for young people. You shouldn't rely on these during your first experiences with intercourse because they require that you and your partner know your bodies extremely well. Also, none prevent sexually transmitted diseases.

spermicides

are chemical substances that kill sperm and prevent them from reaching the uterus. They come in creams or foams and are applied inside the vagina before intercourse.

Spermicide

The Intra-Uterine Device

the intra-uterine device,

or IUD, is a system that a gynecologis inserts into the uterus. It prevents an fertilized ovum from implanting itsel in the uterus. The IUD remains effec- tive for 2 to 3 years.

Don't worry, I bailed out in time...

the diaphragm

is a small ring over which a thin rubber film is stretched. It's prescribed by a doctor, and is placed over the cervix prior to intercourse. It blocks the sperm at the entrance to the uterus. To make it even more effective, it's possible to coat it with a spermicide.

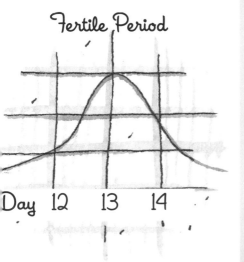

Fertile Period

Day 12 13 14

coitus interruptus

or "pulling out" involves the male removing his penis from the woman's vagina before ejaculation. The problem with this method is that it's hard for men—especially young men—to know far enough in advance when they're going to ejaculate, and to have the will power to pull out before they do. Even if they succeed, a single drop of fluid may drip from the penis before ejaculation takes place, and this one drop contains millions of sperm—certainly enough to fertilize an ovum.

the rhythm method

involves a couple abstaining from intercourse during the time in the woman's menstrual cycle when she is most fertile, that is, during ovulation. This method is not reliable however, because it's difficult to tell exactly when the woman is ovulating. In fact, a woman can be fertile for up to two weeks out of every four-week cycle. It may also be difficult for a couple to resist making love during fertile times.

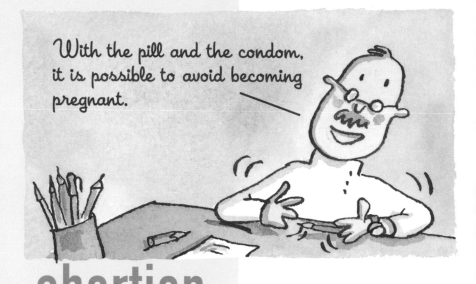

With the pill and the condom, it is possible to avoid becoming pregnant.

abortion

Abortion is not a method of contraception. A woman is already pregnant when she chooses this option, the termination of her pregnancy. When a doctor performs an abortion, he removes the fertilized egg, embryo, or fetus that had begun to develop inside the woman's uterus. In the United States, abortion has been legally permitted since 1973. It is performed safely in hospitals and clinics, such as those run by Planned Parenthood. Girls under eighteen may receive an abortion without telling their parents in some states; in others, they need a parent's or judge's consent. You can contact your local Planned Parenthood health center to find out about the laws in your state, and for more information and counseling about abortions. The Planned Parenthood Web site address is www.plannedparenthood.org.

It's important for a girl or woman to consult a physician or a gynecologist soon after she's made the decision to end her pregnancy, because the procedure becomes more complicated the further along the pregnancy is, and may not be possible after twenty-four weeks. Abortion can be done with an injection and/or pills, or through surgery. No birth control method is 100 percent effective and abortion gives women the ultimate decision of whether or not to become mothers. However, it is a difficult ordeal go through, both physically and emotionally, and by using a contraceptive such as the pill or a condom, the need for an abortion can almost always be avoided.

sexually transmitted diseases

As their name suggests, sexually transmitted diseases (STDs) are spread by intercourse and sometimes even just by contact with a partner's genitals. Some of the most common STDs are chlamydia, gonorrhea, human papilloma virus (HPV), and genital herpes.

chlamydia and gonorrhea are bacterial infections that don't have many early symptoms—sometimes, none at all. Although people who have been infected with either may notice an abnormal discharge from the penis or vagina, or painful urination. If left untreated, these diseases may lead to sterility in women. However they can be easily cured with antibiotics, which is why it's important to see a doctor regularly if you're sexually active, even if nothing's bothering you.

human papilloma virus, or HPV, may also cause no visible symptoms, or it may result in small warts on the penis or at the entrance to the vagina. These can be removed by a surgical operation, as can any pre-cancerous cervical cells HPV can cause in women.

genital herpes appears in men and women as small blisters that form at the entrance to the vagina or the tip of the penis. Before getting this rash, the person feels burning sensations and irritation in the genitals. Various medicines can be prescribed to heal the blisters. However, no treatment can destroy the genital herpes virus, and an infected person may continue to have outbreaks throughout his or her life.

Other STDs often show up as irritations, burning sensations, and abnormal discharges from the penis or vagina. If you experience any of these symptoms, you should see your doctor as soon as possible. Many of these diseases can cause sterility—that is, they can harm your chances of having children—if they aren't treated. A doctor can perform all the appropriate tests and prescribe any necessary medications (usually antibiotics) to keep you healthy.

If you do contract an STD, you are in danger of transmitting the disease to your partner. You'll need to immediately tell the person with whom you're having intercourse, as he or she should be tested and treated as well. If not, your treatment will serve no purpose since your partner, if infected, can pass the infection right back to you.

I buy my own.

isn't there a vaccine? Currently, the only sexually transmitted disease that is preventable with a vaccine is hepatitis B. While most people infected with hepatitis B recover completely, in some it can cause serious liver problems about ten to fifteen years after infection. The hepatitis B virus is also transmitted through blood, and it exists in saliva, so it may be transmitted through activities like kissing or oral sex. If you haven't been vaccinated, ask the advice of your physician, who can administer the vaccine if she feels it's right for you.

A vaccine may soon be available to prevent against HPV, human papilloma virus, as well. Up to 75 percent of adults in the U.S. may have been infected with HPV at some point in their lives. Some infections are fought off by the body's immune system. However, some strains of HPV can lead to cervical cancer in women—in fact, nearly all cases of cervical cancer are caused by HPV. A test called a pap smear, which should be performed regularly by a gynecologist, can catch the early signs of cancer before it develops. Scientists are currently testing an HPV vaccine which, if these tests are successful, could nearly wipe out new cases of cervical cancer altogether.

aids

Human immunodeficiency virus, or HIV, is the virus that causes AIDS (Acquired Immune Deficiency Syndrome). It can pass from one person to another through sexual intercourse. It can also be spread through blood. (That's why it's crucial for drug addicts to never share syringes or needles with each other. A single drop of infected blood in the needle of a syringe is enough to give the virus to another person. For this reason, you should never pick up a syringe that is just lying on the ground somewhere. The tiniest little scratch could cause an infection.)

The AIDS virus attacks the white blood cells, those cells that defend our bodies against all possible infections. People who have AIDS contract many potentially fatal infectious diseases, since they no longer have any defense against germs. In an infected person, AIDS does not appear immediately, even though the virus is present in the blood. At this stage, an infected person is said to be "HIV positive." The only way to know if you are HIV positive is to see your doctor or visit a clinic to have a blood test performed.

Unlike hepatitis B, there is no vaccine against AIDS, and currently *there is no cure*. Medical treatment can slow down the rate at which HIV becomes AIDS and allow victims to live better lives, but it cannot cure them. If you get HIV, you will die of AIDS. Don't be fooled by the posters of the healthy looking HIV-positive people. Medicine may make them feel and look well but they aren't. To avoid getting the AIDS virus, you *must* prevent it from entering your body. The best way to do this is to not have sex, or to use a condom every single time you do. Anyone can get AIDS. Protect yourself.

the condom

Condoms prevent all direct contact between the penis and the vagina. This shield made of rubber blocks the path of any viruses that the man's sperm may harbor. It also blocks the passage of viruses living in the blood or vaginal secretions of the woman to the man. Condoms are, therefore, the only method we have of protecting against AIDS and other STDs other than abstaining from sex altogether. Contrary to what people sometimes believe, a girl who takes birth control pills has no protection against sexually transmitted diseases. That's why even girls who are on the pill need to also use condoms. Beginning with your first sexual experience, using a condom should become a reflex, something you just do, every time you have sex, without having to even think about it.

PROTECT YOURSELF.

use a condom, every time.

desire & intimacy

THE ADVENTURE

listening to your inner voice (and your partner, too)

making love

AS TIME GOES BY

DON'T BE A VICTIM

CONTINUES

knowing how to say NO

there's always
more to learn

Learning about sexuality is like a journey, with all of its discoveries, fears, joys, and disappointments. At the start of the trip, you must be prepared to leave familiar ground and set off in search of your true self, and that of your partner. You must be ready to give and to receive. Don't let a thousand questions or doubts bar the way. You have your whole life in front of you to make the journey a successful one, so avoid taking shortcuts. By trying to grow up too quickly, you could miss a lot of great scenery along the way—or start down the wrong path. You don't want to begin a lifetime of sexuality weighed down by a lot of regrets.

Also, don't feel like you have to immediately uncover the thousand-and-one secrets of sex that you might think adults are harboring. Just begin. Gradually, as you reach, and then move on from, each milestone, you'll be amassing your own body of experience, discovering what gives you pleasure and also what brings pleasure to your partner. Remember: sexuality is a voyage that you make in twos. Each partner must respect the other for the journey to be accomplished in a spirit of joy and affection.

a lifetime of sex

One day, you will have sex for the first time. And then a second time, and a third time. But doing it three times—or even twenty-seven times—doesn't mean you have to keep doing it if at some point you change your mind, or just don't feel like it. It is always your decision, every time, no matter what you've done in the past. Even if you have a happy, fulfilled sex life as an adult, you certain-

No, not tonight.

ly won't have intercourse every day. There'll be times—maybe weeks or months or years—when you won't have sex, because you're not in a relationship, you're too busy at work, you're tired or sick, or because you don't want to.

As a teenager and later, as an adult, your sexual life will be closely connected to your life as a whole, to your encounters, your moments of happiness, and your anxieties. While sex plays a major role in our lives, the goal is to achieve a balance between sexuality and everyday life—in other words, one shouldn't take precedence at the expense of the other. Work and friends and responsibilities shouldn't take up all your time so that there's none left for enjoying loving relationships. At the same time, sex should not be an escape through which you avoid dealing with the responsibilities of life. Sex can be incredibly fulfilling. But it must not be forced. Both partners must want it passionately as part of a relationship built on mutual giving and trust.

don't be a victim

Feelings, sharing, tenderness, dialogue, mutual respect—these are the words you want to describe your sexual experience. But if it's instead marked by threat, pressure, fear, disgust, or humiliation, this is unhealthy, and you must try to free yourself from the situation immediately by telling someone you trust. Rape, pedophilia, and incest are three very serious crimes that the law punishes harshly. Even if you're ashamed to tell anyone what you went through, you have to find the strength to talk about it in order to end your suffering. Remember, if this has happened to you, it is never in any way your fault.

rape

A person commits rape when he or she forces another person, whether through violence or the threat of violence, to have sexual intercourse. It doesn't matter if the victim knows the person, or even if they are on a date when it happens—it's still considered rape if it's against the victim's will. This is a very, very serious crime. If you're raped, you should file a complaint with the police as soon as possible. A doctor will examine you to obtain evidence of the crime, and every effort will be made to try to convict the rapist. Penalties vary from state to state, but a convicted rapist can be sentenced to many, many years in prison.

There are other types of sexual assault besides rape. If an attacker touches a person's genitals or forces that person to touch his or her genitals against his or her will, they have broken the law. In most states, if you're the victim and are under the age of sixteen, this is considered assault even if you didn't say no. Those convicted of sexual assault may also be sentenced to prison. Finally, there are also people called exhibitionists,

who expose their genitals to others, often in public. They are also committing a crime and can be arrested.

pedophilia

Pedophiles are adults who want to have sex with children or teenagers. This is not normal behavior, and if they act on these desires in any way, such as creating or purchasing child pornography, or sexually assaulting a child in the ways described above, it is against the law. Pedophiles are punished similarly to those who commit rape or sexual assault on an adult, but the penalties and prison sentences are more severe. Most states have an "age of consent"—typically 16. Children under this age are not able to legally give their consent to sex or sexual activity, so even if the victim didn't say no or fight the attacker, any sexual contact between an adult and the child is still considered a crime.

incest

When a father or mother has sexual relations with his or her children, he or she is committing incest. Newspapers report more cases of incest between father and daughter, but either parent can commit incest with either a son or a daughter. It can also be committed between close relatives, like an uncle and a niece or a grandfather and granddaughter, or a brother and sister.

Incest is a crime, and those convicted of it will most likely be sent to jail. It is not natural or normal, and has nothing to do with the love a parent feels for his or her child. What's more, in order to persuade the child to have intercourse or to engage in sexual touching, the parent who commits incest often resorts to threats, and sometimes violence. He usually tries to convince the child to keep this all a secret so that he or she will not report the abuse to anyone.

It's very difficult for victims of incest to deal with the fear and shame that it causes. The child may hate the parent for forcing this unwanted sexual attention on him or her, but may also still love and want to protect the abuser, because, after all, he's still one of her parents. To make matters worse, the abused child doesn't always know who to tell about what's been going on, for fear that he or she won't be believed.

Still, it's extremely important that if you have been sexually abused by a family member—or by anyone else for that matter—you tell someone you trust as soon as possible. That might be your other parent or another close relative, a school guidance counselor, or even the police. Otherwise, the situation will likely continue. If the person you tell doesn't take immediate action to end the abuse, tell someone else.

having sex
vs.
making love

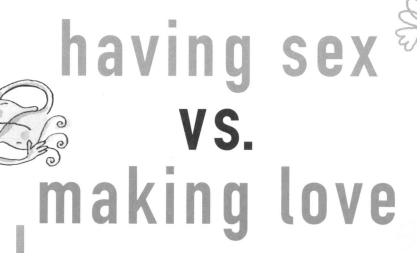

Luckily the discovery of sexuality is often made without going through any dramatic ordeal. Having sex with the person you love and desire can bring true happiness. Love fills life with enchantment; when you're in love, the smallest details of everyday life become wondrous events worthy of celebration. On the other hand, at some point in your life you may choose to have sex with someone you're attracted to, but who you're not hopelessly, madly in love with. This experience may give you physical pleasure, but it can't provide those very, very special sensations that desire and love compounded will bring.

This is why it's important to enjoy sex within a loving relationship. Some people might claim that always making love with the same person is boring. But they're forgetting that when you're with someone you know inside and out, someone who accepts you and loves you for who you are, you're free to explore new ways of experiencing sex that would never be possible with someone brand new to your life. In fact, being in a long-term, loving relationship can often lead to vaster, more pleasurable sexual experiences than having sex with many different partners.

Making love at age forty is different from making love at age twenty. That's why sexuality really is a sort of adventure: all along the way, we're getting to know ourselves, getting to know the opposite sex, and changing and growing as we go. In having a sincere, intimate, sexual relationship with someone, we're revealing our true selves to them—all our strengths and weaknesses, our desires and our fears. Maybe that's why sexuality both frightens and fascinates us at the same time.

But now that you're armed with a wealth of information about both the emotional and physical risks and joys of sexuality, you can go forward confidently, knowing you'll make the decisions that will lead you to greater happiness.

Bibliography

Books

Boston Women's Health Collective. *Our Bodies, Ourselves*. New York: Simon & Schuster, 1984.

Web sites

Adopting.org *www.adopting.org*
The Gay, Lesbian, and Straight Education Network *www.glsen.org*
Columbia University Health Q&A Service *www.goaskalice.columbia.edu*
KidsHealth *www.kidshealth.org*
The Garden of Fertility *www.fertilityawareness.net*
Nebraska Domestic Violence Sexual Assault Coalition *www.ndvsac.org*
Open Adoption and Family Services *www.openadopt.com*
Parents, Families, and Friends of Lesbians and Gays *www.pflag.com*
Planned Parenthood *www.plannedparenthood.com*
Save Roe v. Wade *www.saveroe.com*
Teen Sexuality Information Resources *www.sexuality.about.com/cs/teens*

Articles

Daly, Melissa. "Sex Q & A: 'What Does It Mean if My Pap Smear Comes Back "Abnormal"?'" *Seventeen Magazine* (May 2003), 84.

State of Wisconsin Legislative Reference Bureau, "Sex Crimes and Penalties in Wisconsin," Informational Bulletin 01–1, January 2001.